Table of contents

Released from denial

Erin didn't know what to do. Did she have to wake Luke or not. Until three weeks ago she had never doubted this. Every Sunday, she snuggled against Luke as soon as she was awake. She stroked his muscular chest and enjoyed the touch. Then her hand slid over his tight stomach and finally when she reached his dick, she could already feel that Luke had also woken up. His dick was hard and ready for action. While Erin played with his dick, she felt Luke stroking her butt with his big hands. Occasionally a finger slid through her butt crack. Erin arched her back a bit, so that Luke could reach her pussy better. She enjoyed it intensely when she felt Luke sliding his fingers over her lips and how her pussy slowly got wet. And when her pussy was wet enough, his fingers slid deep inside her. This was the moment that Erin turned around and Luke moved closer to her. From behind his hard dick slid into her pussy and with long strokes he started to fuck her slowly. Erin enjoyed how her orgasm was being built up in a very relaxed way, until she finally came.

Those were the normal Sundays, but the Wednesdays were even better. Every Wednesday Luke and Erin went to the sports club, where they trained for more than an hour. Both of them had their own program, but they made sure that they could see each other all the time. Erin enjoyed seeing Luke train and she was sure he was enjoying it too. There were more than enough exercises in which her ass and legs played the leading role. While Luke was training his biceps, Erin was training her legs. Erin wasn't sure if Luke groaned because of the training or because she kept spreading her legs wide open. During the entire hour Erin turned on her sweetheart and she became more and more horny herself.

At the end of the evening they did an exercise together. They lifted some weights while lying on a couch. If it was very quiet, Erin could not resist teasing Luke a bit. With the barbell in his hands, he couldn't go anywhere. She stroked his shorts until she felt his dick harden. Of course, she knew what would happen when it was her turn. His hand then slid over her shorts and she felt how he put pressure on her pussy. When no one was watching, his hand slid into her pants and she felt his fingers sliding through her wet slit.

After this last exercise, Erin was always very horny. After a quick shower, they had to drive another twenty minutes before they got home. Erin always made sure that she was wearing a short, loose-fitting dress for the return trip. She drove back and tried to keep all the attention on the road, feeling Luke's hand on her bare leg. Sometimes when he was very horny his fingers were already in her pussy before they left the parking garage. The drive home was a game of stopping and continuing. When the playful game became too intense and Erin could no longer keep her attention on the traffic, Luke had to stop. Erin could recover for a short while, but not much later she felt again how his hand slid under her dress. Once home, she was so horny that she wanted to be taken immediately. She often pulled her dress up in the hallway. With spread legs and raised butt, Luke fucked her from behind. After the first lust was gone, they quickly went upstairs. Lying on her back, she spread her legs wide open. While Erin tightly held his muscular, strong body, she felt Luke pumping his hard dick into her tight pussy.

But now, the last three weeks, Luke no longer seemed interested in sex. Erin didn't know why. During the workouts in the gym, Luke reacted lukewarm to her advances. It certainly didn't result in an exciting evening full of sex. At this time, they hadn't had sex for more than three weeks. Erin felt her body becoming more sensitive. Every stroke excited her enormously. While showering she soaked her buttocks and pussy much more than usual. Several times she had been thinking about masturbating, but just then Luke entered the bathroom. After three weeks without sex, she was extremely hot at any time of the day. Just like now, the memories of the Wednesdays had excited her even more than usual. She decided to go for it. She carefully lowered her hand over Luke's chest and felt how strong he was. It excited her even more and she felt how she became wetter. As her hand slowly moved down, she heard Luke wake up. She stopped for a moment. His abdominal muscles felt good. Luke woke up.

"Good morning dear, what a beautiful morning and what a fantastic weather. I have a surprise for you today."

A surprise? Would it happen at last? Would she finally get a good shagging today? Luke moved from under the blanket and sat down on the edge of the bed. In doubt, Erin waited for what would happen. But just like the two weeks before, Luke had other plans this Sunday. Without paying further attention to her, he went to the shower and left her alone. Erin didn't know what to do. She was so horny now that she was thinking of pleasuring herself quickly while Luke was taking a shower. But maybe she should wait. Maybe the surprise was yet to come. She put on a short silk shirt and went to the kitchen. Every Sunday she made a nice breakfast with croissants and eggs to conclude a fantastic morning in bed. Luke sat down fresh and clean, while Erin was still busy in the kitchen. When she took the croissants out of the oven, Erin made sure that she bent over deeply so that Luke had a good view of her buttocks. The shirt was so short that her smooth-shaven pussy had to be clearly visible. Hopefully her wet pussy got Luke excited too.

"Erin, I know what you want for several weeks and I have prepared everything carefully."

This sounded good. All those weeks of waiting were not for nothing.

"What have you prepared for Luke? I am very curious about the surprise."

Luke waited a moment. "Today I'm going to repair the fence. Is that a surprise or not?"

That was certainly a surprise, but not the surprise that Erin had hoped for. She had hoped to feel Luke's big dick deep in her tight pussy. How could Luke suddenly ignore her completely? She wanted to get fucked and couldn't wait any longer. On the other hand, she had asked Luke week after week when he was going to repair the fence. That was finally going to happen. Maybe she should let him go his own way.

Normally they took their time and enjoyed breakfast together, but Luke was in a hurry now and wanted to get started quickly. After breakfast, while Erin placed the dishes in the dishwasher, Luke passed by and stroked her butt.

"Mm, that feels good. Yum."

Before Erin could respond, Luke opened the kitchen door and stepped outside. The gentle touch sparked Erin's sexuality again. Maybe she should touch herself in the bath. After all, the surprise was not what Erin hoped for. She quickly grabbed a few clean towels and filled the tub. From the bathroom she had a good view of the garden. Luke was busy repairing the fence. In the meantime, he had taken off his shirt and was working in his singlet. His trained body was clearly visible. In excitement, Erin stroked her toned body. Her hands ran over her butt and her breasts and she ended between her groins, touching her pussy. How good would it be to feel Luke deep in her again? Her nipples became harder and her clit swelled up. In the meantime, the bath was almost full and Erin stepped into the warm water. The foam hid her body, while her hands slid over her smooth legs and buttocks. As she stroked her entire body, she became more and more excited. She heard again how Luke was working outside. She was so horny now. She wanted more than fingering herself. She wanted to be fucked. She couldn't wait anymore. She got up from the bath and without drying her wet body she walked to the kitchen door and opened it.

"Honey, I beg you to fuck me. I'm so horny now. I need to feel your dick in me. Please fuck me now."

Erin's hand rested on her pussy, with two fingers deep inside it. Luke turned around and smiled.

"I didn't expect you to last so long. Three weeks without sex. It started to become a challenge for me too."

Erin was a little surprised, but now understood that Luke had planned all this. He had let her wait until she was so horny that she would do anything to get fucked. Erin walked through the garden to Luke. She didn't care that she was naked and that the neighbors might see her. She saw that Luke's pants were quite swollen. First, she embraced Luke. Erin was so happy that everything would be all right. His strong hands grabbed her buttocks and slid over her wet, naked body.

"First, let's see how horny you really are. Of course, I can't just simply believe you."

Erin started loosening Luke's belt.

"No, no, that's not what I mean. On the grass."

Erin looked around again and lay down on the grass. She felt the blades of grass tickle in her butt crack. Erin opened her legs wide, put two fingers deep in her wet pussy and started fingering herself.

"Is this horny enough Luke?"

"Go on, you little brat. I'm not convinced yet"

Erin continued to finger and felt how she would soon come to an orgasm. Moaning, she begged Luke: "Honey, I don't want to cum with my fingers. I want you. I want to feel you deep inside me. Please fuck me. Now."

"Then come here."

Erin stood up and snuggled up against Luke. His strong body felt great. While his hands were caressing her body, she loosened his pants and pulled out his hard dick. His dick head gleamed from the precum. As she bent over and lightly touched his dick head with her tongue, she felt how his dick got harder. Erin took his big, hard dick in her mouth and started sucking it. When Luke was about to cum, she stopped.

Luke turned her around and moved her to the fence. Erin leaned against the fence and spread her legs. Luke stood behind her and grabbed her breasts. Her nipples were hard. His hands moved over her belly to her pussy. His fingers slid through her wet lips. Erin arched her back. Luke held her waist and then she felt how he first pushed his dick head between her lips. She moaned loudly as the rest of his hard dick disappeared deep into her pussy. She would finally get fucked. She had waited for this for weeks. Luke pumped her with powerful, deep strokes and soon she felt how a warm load was shot into her pussy. Erin didn't care that it was visible to all neighbors. Moaning with pleasure, she felt a ripping orgasm coming. Her whole body felt sensitive with every touch. That pumping dick in her pussy, she couldn't think of anything else. Shaking on her legs she finally came hard. Erin still felt Luke's hard dick deep in her pussy and they stopped for a moment. Erin looked around with curiosity. It seemed that none of the neighbors had heard or seen them.

She had a great orgasm, but Erin wanted more. She felt insatiable. After three weeks, she wanted to cum more than just once. She turned around.

"Shall we continue in the bedroom, dear? I long for you."

Luke lifted her up and carried her inside. She felt how Luke's spunk ran out of her pussy through her butt crack. The world was beautiful. Luke carried her to the bathroom and turned on the shower. As the warm water flowed over her body and washed everything clean, he knelt before her. He grabbed her butt firmly and pressed his mouth on her pussy. His tongue slid over her still sensitive clit. Erin enjoyed his tongue between her lips and moaned hard as Luke licked her clit. While he ate her out, she could see her moaning clearly excited him. With each moan, his dick became stiffer and harder. It wasn't long before she again had a wonderful orgasm. In the meantime, Luke was so horny that he was about to explode.

Smiling, she grabbed his dick and teasingly pulled it a few times. Luke moaned. Still wet, he lifted her up and brought her to the bedroom, where she was put down on the bed. Immediately Erin turned on her belly and lifted her ass up. Luke crawled on her and pressed his hard cock into her still wet pussy. She was fucked hard for the second time and she enjoyed it to the full. Luke pushed her shoulders onto the mattress. Erin felt how his balls were hitting her pussy, while he fucked her from behind. He groaned and came, shooting a new load of cum in her pussy. Now Erin hadn't had her orgasm and Luke knew that. With two fingers, he thrust deep into her dripping wet cunt, until she finally came too. Exhausted, Erin was recovering. Three times she had a fantastic orgasm and she really wanted to go on, but her body could not.

Not now, but maybe this afternoon.

Tied into submission

Nathalie was grumpy that she had been waiting for half an hour now. It was her birthday today and she still had to go to the office. This morning she had an important meeting and if she had to wait much longer, she would be late. She was well prepared for this meeting. Her career was very important to Nathalie. So important even that she could not give enough attention to Peter, her ex-partner. Eventually, they decided to go their own way and now, after a few months, everything in the house seemed to break. First, Nathalie had tried to fix it herself, but the results were terrible. Frustrated, she had decided to call in a handyman company. She had chosen a company with a motto that appealed to her: "Service with a smile." Nathalie did not know if this was really the best choice, but that didn't matter anymore. Today someone would come over to fix her cupboard, but so far no one had turned up. Nathalie eagerly walked to the kitchen to make a cup of coffee. The doorbell rang exactly when the coffee was ready.

"Yes, that was to be expected. Exactly now."

She quickly walked to the front door. Through the frosted glass of the door, she could see that a fairly large man was standing on the sidewalk. She opened the door and saw that he was tall and muscular. "Mm, yummy," was the first thing she thought.

"Good morning, I am Erik and I am here to repair a cupboard"

"Good morning, you are quite late. I hope you can work fast, because I have to be at the office in time."

"I don't expect it to be a problem, but maybe I can see the cupboard first?"

They went upstairs together, Nathalie leading the way. As she climbed the stairs, Nathalie felt how Erik was looking at her butt. Her neat office pants were tight around her buttocks. Immediately, she felt a lot better. It was always good to notice that men thought she was good-looking and sexy. Nathalie noticed that she rocked her hips a little more than usual. The cupboard was in the bedroom and normally all her clothes hung in it, but now they were scattered on the bed. The bar on which the clothes normally hung had come off and lay on the bottom of the cupboard.

"That is a sturdy bar, but the mounting is not very solid. I can do something about it. I have to get some tools."

Together they walked down again. While Erik grabbed his tools, Nathalie took her coffee from the kitchen. She was impressed by Erik's looks. He was tall, muscular and very sexy. Distracted, she had almost forgotten that she had little time. She quickly glanced at her watch. Even less time than she thought.

"Please, let me know if I can help. The sooner it is finished the better"

"Thank you. I think you can help. I'll let you know when I need you."

Erik went upstairs and Nathalie started to read the minutes of the previous meeting. It took quite a long time for Erik to call her up. She quickly went upstairs. She saw that there were now two very strong brackets in the cupboard.

"Good, I was afraid that you would not make it in time," she said, somewhat grumpier than she actually meant.

"Well, in that case, we'll have to do the rest a bit quicker. If you hold this bar, I'll get the screws and the tools."

While Nathalie was holding the bar above her head, Erik turned the screws on both sides into the brackets.

"Just hold on. I have to do something."

"Are you not ready yet?"

Erik leaned over Nathalie with a roll of duct tape.

"Can you move your hands closer together please?"

Meekly, Nathalie moved her hands together and looked questioningly.

"Is this ok?"

"Yes, that is fine."

'Ritz, ratz', with a quick movement, Erik had wrapped a long strip of duct tape around her hands and the bar. Nathalie couldn't go anywhere anymore.

"What is the meaning of ..."

'Ritz, ratz', before she had finished speaking, he had also put a strip of duct tape on her mouth. Nathalie looked anxiously at Erik. What was he up to? This didn't promise any good.

"Look at you, such a grumpy lady. I guess you haven't enjoyed a good shagging for a long time."

Nathalie couldn't believe what she heard. Was he going to abuse her? Here, in her own house? In panic, she pulled at the bar with all her force, but it didn't give in. Erik was clearly a professional.

"Such a beautiful body definitely qualifies for some extra service," smiled Erik.

Nathalie looked around anxiously. She couldn't go anywhere, but she wouldn't just give in. The karate lessons now came in handy. As soon as Erik approached, Nathalie kicked in his direction. She almost hit him.

"Oh, a wild cat. I better be careful."

Every time Erik came closer, Nathalie kicked, but at one point she got tired and eventually Erik managed to grab one of her legs. She tried to pull back, but before she knew it, her leg was taped to the bed. There she stood, with her legs spread, standing on one leg. She anxiously waited for what would happen. Erik came closer and placed his hand on her cunt.

With her legs spread, he could easily reach it. She felt how his hand rubbed her pussy through the fabric of the pants.

Then he massaged her breasts through her slim-fit blouse. Erik did not bother to unbutton her blouse. He slowly ripped her blouse open. One by one the buttons came loose and he got a view of her white lace bra.

"Very nice. Very nice, I am curious what I will find below."

His strong hands slid over her toned body and pushed up the bra. Erik took her firm breasts in his hands and touched her nipples. He leaned over and licked her nipples until they became stiff. Then his hands went down and her pants were unbuttoned. The zipper slid down and showed her white lace panties.

"Mm, what a horny panties you put on to work. I guess, your boss is happy with that."

Erik's hand slid into her panties and Nathalie felt one of his fingers slide into her pussy.

"You are ready. It is time to service you."

Erik went to his toolbox, fiddled around and came back with scissors. Without much effort, he cut open one of her legs from top to bottom. One buttock was now clearly visible. Before Erik continued, he grabbed her butt firmly. She felt how his hand covered her entire buttock. He quickly cut open the other trouser leg and her pants fell to the floor.

He quickly cut off her blouse and bra. With her legs spread, Nathalie was wearing only her lace panties. His hand slid into her panties and she felt how he rubbed her clit and pressed a finger between her pussy lips. Eventually, Erik also cut the panties loose.

"This will be a pleasant memory later," and he threw the clipped panties on the bed.

He sat down between her legs and came face to face with her pussy. Nathalie felt his tongue touching her clit. She didn't want to and struggled against it. Immediately, she felt how he firmly held her buttocks and pressed her pussy to his mouth. Nathalie couldn't stop it happening, her struggling was effortless. His wet tongue slid through her lips. She didn't want to get excited. How could she get excited while he was abusing her, but she couldn't stop her body from reacting? She noticed how her pussy was getting wet from the touching. He would probably misunderstand this.

"I can already taste that you enjoy it, just like Lisa told me."

Just as she thought, he thought she enjoyed being abused. But what did he say: "Just like Lisa told me"? What did Lisa have to do with this? Lisa was her best friend. They shared everything and sometimes they had shared their sexual desires and fantasies. More than once, Nathalie had said that she fantasized about being fucked while tied up. Would this have been arranged by Lisa; as a present for her birthday? What should she do now, enjoy it or not?

Erik was still licking her pussy and Nathalie felt how he slowly was pushing her to an orgasm.

"Doubt? Continue or stop?"

Nathalie doubted and shook no, but Erik didn't stop.

"I don't believe you. I see you enjoy it. I can do better. I have something here that made many customers very happy."

Erik felt in his pocket for a moment and Nathalie watched as he pulled out a string with five beads.

"You will love this. I am sure."

Then she felt how he pressed the first bead against her butt hole. Nathalie moaned softly as Erik slowly pushed all the five beads into her arse.

"Good, you are so much sweeter this way."

How could she stop this and did she want to stop it? Not really. He was doing so well; he must have been hired. After all, he said he made many customers happy. And does a normal handyman take a string with anal beads to work; Nathalie doubted it? She wanted to believe that Erik was her birthday present, arranged for her by Lisa. This felt so good. She gave in and enjoyed his touches.

She felt how he went on. His fingers slipped in and out of her wet slit, while his tongue licked her clit. She was about to cum. And then, he stopped.

" I can see you enjoy this, but I also want to have some fun."

He quickly took off his shirt and pants. His shorts were tight and Nathalie could see how excited Erik was. A big hard dick stood straight up when he lowered his shorts. He came to stand behind her and she felt his hand slide from her belly to her pussy. She bent over as far as she could and Erik's dick slipped into her wet pussy. His firm hands held her waist. While he smacked her ass, she arched her back so that he got even deeper into her.

"Even hornier than I thought. You wanted this all the time, isn't it?"

Nathalie moaned and hoped that Erik was indeed ordered, but it didn't matter anymore. She was getting fucked, as she hadn't been fucked for a long time. Erik kept on thrusting his long, hard dick in her tight pussy and it didn't take long before she felt her orgasm build up again, much more intense than before. She felt how Erik pulled at the string. One by one he slowly pulled a few beads out of her arse. This pushed her over the edge. Moaning of pleasure and shaking on her legs, Nathalie was having her best orgasm ever. Erik stopped and looked satisfied how she had cum. Then he grabbed her hips again and bend Nathalie over. His hard dick was thrust into her wet pussy again and he started to pump her hard. Not much later Nathalie felt how he shot his warm load into her pussy. He kept on thrusting until his dick got softer.

While Erik was putting on his clothes and tidying up his tools, Nathalie still hung on the bar and felt his cum run from her pussy down her legs. She enjoyed her fantasy, but why did he let her hang here?

"I can't stay longer. The next job is waiting. I have to go, but before I do, I would almost forget something," Erik smiled and pulled the last two anal beads out of her butt hole. Nathalie panted.

Then, Erik cut one of her hands loose. She quickly pulled the duct tape from her mouth. Doubt struck. He gave her the scissors.

"Wait, don't go yet. Stay here."

Erik was already on his way down. When Nathalie cut herself loose, she heard Erik drive away. She quickly searched her phone among the clipped clothes. She pressed Lisa's number. It only took a while before Lisa answered.

"Hi Lisa, did you arrange a surprise for me?"

"Yes. How do you like them? Aren't they beautiful flowers?"

"Flowers? Just a bunch of flowers?"

"Yes, a bunch of flowers with a card."

Quickly, Nathalie ran downstairs, opened the front door, and saw a bunch of flowers with a card in it: "Happy Birthday, Lisa." Her clipped panties lay on top of the bunch of flowers. Nathalie smiled, a pleasant memory indeed.

Strip poker at the office

Last week Denise won the poker tournament easily. What will happen this week, now her opponents know her strengths? Will she win or does she have to accept defeat?

Chapter 1

Last week Denise won the tournament easily. What will happen this week?

"Denise, last week you played so well. I didn't expect you to win so gloriously. Why didn't you tell us that you're such a good poker player? Do you think you want to play again tonight?"

Denise didn't have to think long about this. Last week she won the tournament and with it 200 dollars. Although it was the first time she had played poker at the office, it was certainly not the first time she had played poker. Her colleagues were not prepared for this and they had grossly underestimated her p. She had fully exploited the advantage and 3 hours later she won all the chips of her colleagues; twenty colleagues, including three other female colleagues, who did not know the poker rules, but played merely for fun of it.

Tonight, Denise had to be careful. Her colleagues knew her talents now and she wouldn't win as easy as last time. She needed something to impress her colleagues. Something that would make it clear that she would win again tonight. The 200 dollars she won last week should be enough to buy something that could do the job.

The morning had passed quickly, on Fridays it was always quieter. All of a sudden Denise knew what she would buy from the prize money, a sexy dress that would take her colleagues out of their concentration. Fortunately, it was just lunchtime. She quickly went to a fancy clothing store, where she expected to find a nice dress. She quickly searched the racks, but couldn't find anything that quickly. A young woman approached her.

"Can I help you, ma'am?"

"Sure, I'm looking for something sexy that radiates victory. I have a poker tournament tonight and I want to make it clear I am the one that is going to win it."

"Sure, I think we have something fits the bill. I have a beautiful mini dress here that seems to be made of silk, but it is elastic and fits tightly around the body. I have different colors, but I think black would look stunning with your blonde hair."

When Denise fitted the dress, she immediately felt how comfortable it was. The fabric was very light and smooth, like a second skin. What she saw in the mirror was even better. Her butt in particular looked great. She only had to buy other underwear, because this was too visible. On the way out, she grabbed a G-string and a new bra that promised not be visible and paid the bill.

The break was just over when she arrived at the office. Satisfied with her purchases, she went back to work. Just like the morning, the afternoon passed by quietly and before she knew it was five o'clock.

Denise decided to change into her new dress first and then eat something. That way she could immediately see if the dress had the desired effect. Changing clothes in the toilet was a bit tricky, but not much later she had her new dress on. When she looked in the mirror, she was shocked to see that the G-string was more visible than her other panties. She turned around a few times, but had to accept it, this didn't look good at all. The mini dress fitted nicely over her butt, but the G-string was clearly too visible. After some hesitation, Denise decided not to wear the G-string. She looked at herself again in the mirror. This looked good, exactly as she had hoped. Fortunately, the bra was all right. Luckily, she didn't have to show up in her mini dress with her nipples piercing through the fabric.

The mirror in the elevator showed Denise again how hot she looked. The idea that she went into town without wearing a string excited her.

Arriving outside, the sun was shining pleasantly on her skin. She didn't have to walk far to the sandwich shop, but with every step her dress crawled up a little. Every ten steps she had to pull the dress down again to prevent her butt from becoming visible. In the clothing store she had not realized this, because she had not been walking around, but now it was a bit of a problem. Fortunately, Denise didn't have to walk when playing poker tonight.

Denise bought two sandwiches and a cup of coffee and paid the bill. As she walked back, she suddenly realized that she no longer had her hands free to pull her dress down. The cool breeze between her legs made clear that it was actually really necessary now. She quickly stopped to prevent the mini dress form sliding up even further and bend over to place the cup of coffee on the footpath. While leaning forward, the dress slipped up and showed her bare ass to the public. A young man, walking right behind her, smacked her bare butt and walked on laughing. With a red head, she quickly pulled down her dress, left her coffee, and made it quickly to the office.

When she arrived at the office, she ate the sandwiches and realized that the dress had certainly attracted attention. Hopefully it would help her tonight.

Denise was right in time when she entered the canteen. She could clearly see that everyone had noticed her entry. The male staff in particular seemed very interested. Her goal was achieved. With less concentration, they would play worse and give Denise more chance to win again.

"I bought this dress from the previous prize and I have already set my eyes on another one that I will buy from tonights' prize.", she joked.

"If you keep coming in such horny dresses you can win all the time.", Ed smiled.

Denise did not expect this, but she secretly enjoyed the attention. Fortunately, she did not blush and she could stay cool, otherwise all the effort would have been wasted.

After everyone had grabbed a drink and found their place at the right table, the tournament started. It didn't take long for Denise to take the lead again and after two hours she was already playing at the final table with only Ed. The rest of the staff was anxiously watching who would win. Ed had considerably more chips and Denise thought that thorough measures were needed.

"Can we take a little break, Ed? I have to go to the bathroom."

Without waiting for the answer, she got up and headed for the toilets. As she knew, her dress would slide up a little with every step, and when Denise reached the door, her butt was almost visible. The male staff started whistling. Just before she reached the door, she smoothed the dress. In the toilet she took off the bra. Denise felt the soft fabric on bare breast and her nipples and she felt how it aroused her. Her nipples hardened and pierced through the thin fabric. This would certainly cause distraction.

When Denise sat down again, the change had not gone unnoticed. Ed had a good view of her breasts and could certainly see her stiff nipples.

"Your dress looks even better this way, are you sure you don't have to walk a little longer? Maybe you have to go to the toilet again?"

"No, no," Denise laughed. "But I can still use a drink."

She stood up and went to the bar. The distance was a little further than to the door. She slowly took every step, rocked her hips a little and enjoyed the looks of the colleagues. Just before she reached the bar, she smoothed the dress. When she turned around, she saw the disappointed looks. The way back, Denise moved just as defiantly but let her dress crawl up until she reached the table. Her pussy was just not visible. She heard colleagues moan softly and Ed was visibly excited too.

Denise won the next game easily, but Ed was not so easily defeated and again he won a few more games. This required more action. On purpose Denise knocked over a pile of her chips, which ended on the floor. She quickly crawled under the table. Her dress tightened even more around her butt and she felt how the fabric even pressed against her pussy. This had to be a beautiful sight for her colleagues, but it didn't help to upset Ed. She came out from under the table, went over to his side and crawled back under the table again. Now he had to have a very good view. She arched her back a bit so that her butt was even more visible.

Suddenly she felt a hand go over her pussy and butt, one or two fingers sliding through her butt-crack. She didn't expect that Ed dared to do this with all the colleagues around.

"That beautiful ass begged to be touched, don't you think guys?"

All the colleagues laughed and with a blush on her cheeks, Denise quickly came out from under the table. Anyway, she had all her chips back.

Chapter 2

The tournament runs not as expected. Can Denise handle the stress?

Out of concentration, Denise lost the next hand and with it the tournament. Ed was 200 dollars richer. Afterwards, the tournament and especially Denise's tactics were extensively discussed while enjoying even more drinks and nibbles. During the evening, most colleagues left home. Somewhat drunk, Ed came to her.

"I would have let you win if I had known for sure that you would show up in such a sexy dress next time."

The other two remaining colleagues could only confirm this. Even Juliet, her female colleague, had to admit that the dress was very sexy. She herself had also done her best. Her beautiful figure came out well in a tight shirt and skinny jeans.

"I want to give you another chance to win your money back, but then we'll play a different variant of poker."

Before she knew it, Denise had already agreed because she wanted revenge.

"The atmosphere is so good now and Denise has warmed us up quite well. What do you think of a game of strip poker with the four us?"

Juliet and Frank looked up somewhat surprised. The men quickly agreed that they thought this was a good idea. Juliet and Denise had their reservations.

"Please, let us think for a moment."

These colleagues were beautiful, well-groomed men, who both looked very handsome. Ed had already made it clear that he an eye on Denise. In addition, Denise hadn't had a partner for a long time and Juliet was already quite drunk and in for a joke. Denise mainly wanted her money back, but an affair with Ed was certainly not a punishment. She had enjoyed his attention all evening.

"All right, we have made up our mind. We want to play too."

Ed explained: "Let's discuss the rules first. We all start with an equal number of clothing. Clothing that is taken off cannot be put on again. The person with the lowest hand loses and must hand in an item of clothing or can play 'Truth or Dare'."

This sounded exciting and Denise was increasingly looking forward to this game of poker. They all started to count the number of clothing they were wearing. Frank and Ed were wearing five items of clothing. Juliet also had five pieces of clothing on, a tight shirt and jeans, underwear and boots.

"When I put my heels on again, I'll end up with only two items of clothing," Denise confessed.

"I already thought I could see and feel that," Ed grinned.

"Ok, let me think. If we three take off one piece of clothing and you use two of us, then we are start equally."

Frank and Ed quickly took off their shirts, showing their muscular chests. Juliet decided to take off her boots. Denise started the game with two extra shirts.

The game didn't start well. Ed won the first two rounds with flying colors, so Frank had to hand in his pants and Juliet her t-shirt. Her beautiful, toned figure was even more visible now. The next round Ed lost, his shoes and socks were won by Frank. Now, he was sitting at the table in just his pants. Juliet only wore her briefs, but she did her very best to lose them quickly. During the game her hands regularly disappeared under the table and it was clear that her briefs were obstructing her actions. Frank also had only his boxers on and he was clearly excited by the horny Juliet. Every now and then his hand disappeared under the table and a moment later Juliet started to moan. This made it difficult for Denise and Ed to focus on the game. Denise had three pieces of clothing to use. Ed had two more.

With a little too much bravado, Denise played the following games and lost a shirt and her heels. Now she only had her mini dress left. Fortunately, she could also play for 'Truth or Dare' so that she would not immediately lose her dress. Frank and Juliet each had an extra item of clothing. The cards were shuffled and Denise got two Aces. With this she had to be able to win. A King, a Ten and Two, were on the table. She should be able to win this round. Ed didn't pass. The next card was a Queen. Denise was full of confidence. Two Aces was still more than two Kings and the chance of a Street was still present. The last card was a Queen and it completed Ed's 'Three of a Kind'. Denise lost and had to admit defeat. Lucky she could still play the game of 'Truth and Dare'.

Ed asked: "Truth or Dare?"

Denise was in for a joke, what could happen.

"Let's do 'Dare'."

"Ok, Denise, do you dare to touch my boxer shorts?"

Denise had not yet expected this, but without doubt she walked over to Ed and rubbed the boxer shorts until his dick clearly swelled up and the head became visible. Denise grinned when she sat down again.

The next hand Frank beat Juliet. Inspired by Ed, Frank asked if Juliet dared to touch his dick. Without hesitation, Juliet walked over to Frank, leaned forward, took his dick out and licked his dick head a few times.

"You didn't say what I could touch it with," said Juliet daringly.

The cards were dealt again and now Denise won.

"Truth or Dare?"

As expected, Ed chose 'Dare'.

"Do you dare...", Denise turned her back to Ed and raised her butt. "...to stroke my ass?"

Before she knew she felt a hand disappear under her dress and two fingers slid into her pussy.

"I said my ass not my pussy, Ed."

Ed quickly pulled his hand back and instead stroked her ass. All the touching made Denise quite horny and she wished that Ed hadn't pulled back his hand so quickly.

Denise wanted to lose the next game, so she could take off her new dress. Effortlessly, she lost the game. She stood up and slowly pulled up her dress. Little by little her shaven pussy became visible to everyone. After this, she stripped down further, slowly exposing her breasts, until she was completely naked. She moved her hands over her body, from her breasts to her belly, to her butt and then to the front, where she ended up between her groins.

"Denise, I am getting very hot here. Sorry, but I have to take off my panties."

Juliet placed her wet panties on the table and sat down again. Frank and Ed followed immediately. Now, everyone was sitting naked at the table. All games would now be played with 'Truth and Dare'.

The following game Ed lost again.

"Truth or Dare?"

Denise didn't have to think long and was in the mood for something more daring.

"Do you dare..."

She got up, put her hands on the table, spread her legs and raised her ass.

"...to stick your finger in my ass?"

Ed came to stand behind her and she felt how he placed his hands on her butt, stroking them and then grabbing them firmly. His hands moved down her legs, caressing them and then back up to her butt. This felt so good. Two fingers slid through her butt-crack. Denise relaxed in anticipation of what was going to happen.

"Come on, or don't you dare?", she asked provocatively.

"Yes, come on Ed, you can do it," Frank encouraged Ed.

Denise felt how Ed's hands moved to her waist and then to her breasts. He squeezed them and played with her stiff nipples.

"I can feel you're horny now, aren't you? You bad girl."

Denise could not deny this. She enjoyed the caresses and felt how she got wetter. Ed's hands moved back to her butt. Denise arched her back and pushed her ass further backwards. A hand slid between her legs and she felt Ed moved closer to her.

"Come on then, Ed."

Denise felt how something warm slid through her butt-crack and before she realized it, Ed had pushed his hard dick into her wet slit. She didn't expect it, but secretly hoped it, and she couldn't hide that she enjoyed it very much. She moaned with pleasure with every thrust and then Ed placed his thumb on her butt-hole.

"This, this is what you wanted. Isn't it, Denise?"

"Yeah, yeah, please do it."

Ed pressed his thumb into her asshole. Denise wanted this to never stop. While fucking her from behind, he spanked her ass, and god did she like it. She felt that Ed was coming and she contracted her inner muscles to become even tighter.

"Oh, you naughty girl, you feel so good.", Ed groaned. Denise felt how a warm load was shot into her pussy. While Ed was recovering, his dick was still hard and deep in her. Denise craved to cum and started to slide back and forward over his stiff cock, while she rubbed her clit. Just as she nearly reached her orgasm, Ed pulled his dick out of her wet pussy.

"Just be patient, my little slut, you will get the first prize soon."

Chapter 3

Denise has to accept defeat, but really enjoys it.

How cruel, she was so horny now that she would do anything to cum. Denise saw how Juliet sat on Frank's lap. Sitting with her back to him, she rode his dick fiercely, completely in control. Franks hands moved from Juliet's tits to her pussy and Juliet moaned intensely. After a few minutes, she was almost screaming out loud when she reached her orgasm.

Denise felt envious. Everyone had had an orgasm, except for her. Under the table she secretly started to rub her clit. She began to breathe heavily and couldn't hide that she was almost cumming. Quickly Ed came to her and grabbed her hands.

"I thought I told you that you will receive the first prize soon."

He took Denise's dress off the floor and he tied her hands on her back with it.

Ed spoke to others: "I suggest that we adjust the rules of our card game a bit more. Anyone who wins a hand can spoil this horny little lady, but if she cums you lose. The one who remains will get the 200 dollars I won earlier."

Frank and Juliet happily agreed with the new rules. Denise wanted to protest, but she was horny and got excited about the idea to be sexually spoiled.

The cards were dealt and Juliet won the first round. She asked Denise to lie on the floor and spread her legs. Denise listened meekly. Juliet knelt before her and Denise felt Juliet's tongue disappear between her lips. As a woman, Juliet knew exactly what felt good and she wanted Denise to enjoy it. Passionately, her tongue slid between Denise's lips and over her clit. Denise went wild.

"Yes, yes, deeper please," Denise pleaded.

Juliet obeyed and stuck her tongue deeper in Denise's wet pussy. She moved it in and out repeatedly but when she noticed that Denise was about to cum, she stopped abruptly.

"No, don't stop. Please, go on. I beg you, please. You can't do this to me. I was about to cum, hard. Go on. Please."

It didn't matter how Denise begged, Juliet wanted to win the money and left her lying on floor. All three of them enjoyed how Denise was yearning to be touched.

Again, the cards were dealt and now Frank won. After the extensive licking that had just taken place, not much was needed to make Denise cum. Frank understood this too. He massaged Denise's breasts and butt and his hands slid between her groins, touching her pussy. With every touch, Denise moaned intensely and she saw how Frank got excited, as his dick got harder and bigger. Denise wanted to encourage him to fuck her. She took his dick in her mouth and started to suck it. Before she knew he came in her mouth. When she swallowed his cum, she felt sluttish and it she felt good about it. It aroused her even more. She was so horny. Desperately, she tried to touch her pussy, but the bondage made this impossible. She couldn't do anything else than wait for the outcome of the next hand.

When Juliet won the next hand, Denise wasn't cooled down a bit. Juliet asked her to lie down again for another oral treat. The idea alone made Denise almost cum. Juliet took her place between Denise's legs. Juliet touched Denise's breasts, licked her nipples and kissed her way to her pussy. When she arrived there, she stuck her tongue between Denise's lips and began to lick her again. On hands and knees Juliet's ass looked gorgeous. Ed had seen this too and he placed himself behind her, grabbed her ass and slid two fingers deep into her cunt. Juliet moaned and lost her attention to Denise. She arched her back to make her wet pussy even more accessible. Ed slid in and out of her soggy cunt with two fingers. Juliet moaned with pleasure when she came. She leaned forward and lay down on Denise. She kissed Denise and stroked her breasts and belly as she recovered from her orgasm.

Ed gently pushed Juliet aside.

"Turn over, Denise. I have got a surprise for you."

Willingly Denise turned on her stomach and heard how Ed ran to his desk on the same floor. Again, Denise tried hard to push her fingers into her hot pussy, but it was impossible.

"I bought this present for my girlfriend, but I think you will enjoy it just as much."

Before Denise could see what Ed meant, he had already sat down behind her.

"Face down, ass up, Denise."

Denise crawled on her knees. Raising her ass, she immediately felt something slide over her pussy. Then she felt a slight vibration and realized what Ed had brought. Slowly the vibrator slipped into her pussy. Then she felt something press against her butt hole that also started vibrating.

"How does this feel, Denise?"

Denise gave a gasping reply: "More, more, this is feels so good."

The shaft started to rotate and some beads inside the vibrator started to rotate too. She felt how Ed pushed the vibrator deeper in her pussy and then she felt some vibration against her clit. All her holes were filled and all her sensitive spots were being touched. Denise had never felt so much pleasure. It was almost too much for her. Ed adjusted the vibrator slightly differently. The shaft started to rotate a little faster, and also the beads were vibrating faster.

"How is this?"

"Yes, please let it go."

Denise felt how her clit was massaged and how an orgasm was quickly building up. Ed started to move the vibrator in and out of her pussy to give Denise even more pleasure.

"Don't move it, this is divine. Leave it there."

The vibrator buzzed and vibrated in her pussy and ass while Ed watched. Denise came, moaning of pleasure. With the vibrating vibrator still in her pussy, she laid down on her stomach. Ed adjusted the vibrator so that it turned around very quietly and released her hands again. Denise turned on her side and pulled the vibrator out of her pussy.

"This was so good. Would you like to lay next to me now, Ed?"

Both on their sides Ed lay behind her. While Ed stroked her body, Denise pressed her ass against Ed's dick. She wanted more. She wanted to cum again. It wasn't long before she felt how Ed's cock was getting harder between her butt crack. Denise wiggled her ass a bit and Ed's dick slipped into her wet slit. This was, by far, her favorite position and she enjoyed how he worked his hard dick in her tight pussy while massaging her breasts at the same time. For the second time she had an overwhelming orgasm.

Fully satisfied Denise smiled; she saw that there was not much left of her new dress. It was completely ruined and out of shape. To buy a new one, she would have to join the tournament again next week.